STOP IN THE NAME OF LOVE

BOOK 1 OF THE SUGAR SERIES

NALEIGHNA KAI
U. M. HIRAM

MACRO PUBLISHING GROUP

Macro Publishing Group

The Macro Group, LLC

Stop in the Name of Love © 2023 by Naleighna Kai and U. M. Hiram

Cover designed by: Woodson Creative Studio

Interior design by: Woodson Creative Studio

Find Naleighna Kai on the web at www.naleighnakai.com

And U. M. Hiram at https://authorumhiram.com/

EBOOK ISBN: 9781952871511

ACKNOWLEDGMENTS

Special thanks goes out to: The Creator from whom all Blessings and opportunities flow, Sandy (my true mother), my son, J. L. Woodson (for the awesome cover designs for this Merry Hearts series), Sesvalah, Bettye Odom, Janice M. Allen, Debra J. Mitchell, Royce Slade Morton, Bunny Ervin, J. L. Campbell, Kelly Peterson, Janine A. Ingram, Ehryck F. Gilmore, Betty Clawson, Jamyi Joy, Stephanie M. Freeman, Unique Hiram, Marie L. McKenzie, Shawn Williams, Dr. Vanessa Howard, the Kings of the Castle Ambassadors, Members of Naleighna Kai's Literary Cafe, the members of NK's Tribe Called Success, the members of Namakir Tribe, and to you, my dear readers . . . thank you all for your support.

U. M. HIRAM

First and foremost, I would like to thank God for the gift and talents that he has given me as well as continuing to answer my prayers. He has been opening doors and placing some amazing people in my life.

Naleighna Kai, thank you for the vision that you have and giving me the opportunity to share this literary space with you. Your coaching and mentorship mean so much to me and I feel blessed to be on this journey with you.

Jenise, Malcolm, and Brandon – what can I say? Thank you for the continued support, understanding, and cheering me on through this writing life. You are an amazing sister, son, and nephew. Love you all with everything in me.

Tribe Called Success, I appreciate each and every one of you for embracing and encouraging me through this surreal journey. I am excited for all that is in store for us. It's about to be lit ya'll!

Readers, Book Reviewers, Beta Readers - know that none of this would not be possible without the support you give authors through your feedback, purchases, and spreading the word about our books. Putting pen to paper is not always easy, but each of you help to make this literary life worth it.

CHAPTER 1

"$\mathcal{W}$hen did policemen start looking like *that?*" Elise Payne gasped, putting a tighter grip on the steering wheel.

She had been pulled over for speeding, but she couldn't believe that someone as breathtaking as Officer Friendly had stepped out of the cruiser. The man had expressive, dark brown eyes and smooth golden features—a proud nose and sensuously curved lips—carved into a ruggedly handsome face that was damn pleasant to look at along with a muscular body that was nothing but pleasure to watch. Elise normally enjoyed milk chocolate, but maybe it was time to give vanilla bean some consideration.

The fact that this delay would probably make her miss the train slipped her mind as she became totally smitten by the most handsome male since Jesus turned water into wine. She could picture those gorgeous lips doing wicked, forbidden things to her—the kind of things that made a woman start speaking in tongues, the kind of things that made a woman leave religion at the altar and dive headfirst into temptation, skinny dip in an overdose of sin, and—

"License, insurance, and registration, ma'am."

Her fantasy circled the bowl and flushed right down the drain with those words. She let out a long, slow breath and said, "May I take my hands off the steering wheel?"

He nodded, grimacing as he did so.

Elise inched her hand into her satchel and produced a license, then leaned toward the glove compartment and froze at the thoughts whipping through her mind. *Registration, no problem. Insurance, huuuuge problem. Expired. Five hundred dollars.*

She tried to keep the despair from showing on her face as she slid the documents to him. Elise watched his every move as he walked back to his cruiser at a snail's pace.

Seriously? Can't you go any faster?!

Several minutes ticked by before he returned. She quickly put her hands on the wheel before he made it all the way to the driver side window.

This time, he sighed with impatience. "It's safe to take your hands off the wheel, Ms. Payne. I'm a Burnham officer. It's the Chicago police who are trigger-happy."

Elise remained completely silent. Maybe if she zipped her lips, he would give her the ticket and let her be on her damn way.

"Do you realize you were going 77 in a 45?" he asked.

"Actually, I thought it was just 65, but 77 it is," she shot back.

He paused for a moment, his right eyebrow lifting. Elise saw a sudden slight uplift at the corners of his lips. There was a fullness that made them the most kissable pair she'd seen in a long time. What was it about this man's lips that invited her to give him a second and third look? What was it about those dark brown eyes that held a sparkle of mischief, but a smidgen of pain behind them? And how was that so easy for her to recognize?

"*Why* were you going so fast?" he asked.

"Because I was trying to catch that train *riiiiight* there," she replied, gesturing to the silver and orange commuter whizzing past them on a black bridge overhead. Her heart sank. All hopes of landing that new position were gone.

"There'll be another one coming along."

The train disappeared from their view, and she returned her focus to him. "Not in enough time to make it downtown for my first day." She slumped in the leather seat and whispered, "And this one had a chance to go permanent."

The officer looked down at her, as though summing things up, summing *her* up. "Well, I'm not going to ticket you for speeding."

Her grateful gaze locked on him.

"Or for the fact that you weren't wearing a seatbelt."

She opened her mouth to protest that she had only slipped it off because he had taken so long, but shut it and nodded her thanks.

"Or for the fact that your insurance expired last week."

"Thank you, Officer Montgomery," she murmured as he slid the items back to her. Their hands touched briefly, and a jolt of electricity whipped through her. She looked up in time to see his shocked expression. *Ah, he felt it too.*

At that moment, however, the only electricity she needed to worry about was ComEd. Her lights and power were about to become a distant memory if she didn't dance into their office with something more than a handful of "give me" and a mouthful of "much obliged."

"This picture," Officer Montgomery said, gesturing to a photo of her with her sister where they both wore black hats--derbies or Dobbs as her grandmother called them. The smiles were from a happier time when they went to a mystery dinner and played detective. They were the only ones to solve the murder that evening and were awarded those special hats by the event hosts. Strangely enough, her ex had been mean enough to take those with him, knowing how much they meant to her.

She explained this to the officer, and a sadness came over those dark brown eyes before he tipped his hat. "So sorry to hear that. You have a nice day, ma'am. And leave a little earlier next time."

When he walked back to the cruiser, Elise laid her forehead on the steering wheel. Tears she had been holding back for months finally had their reign. The energy to forge on, to get up and dust herself had never abandoned her—but everything happening at once had finally taken its toll.

Elise moaned as the tears increased. Her entire life was at a standstill, and most wasn't of her own making. All of her money was gone. Every single dime she had had been used to keep her twin sister alive, only to lose that beautiful soul to kidney and liver failure last month.

No sooner than she could breathe again without razor blades tearing into her lungs from that loss, did her rich ex-husband swoop down with a team of lawyers and manage to steal her baby boy while she was distracted with grief and the fallout of her family's displeasure at what she'd done to keep her sister alive as long as she could. Yet, she had gathered up whatever resources she could, fought with everything she had, only to lose her son, anyway.

Another blow, another setback, another harsh, bitter loss. The last being the one which left her so out of sorts—at least financially. The fact that Ameritech's merger put her and 5,000 other people on the unemployment line was a wakeup call that blared in her ears every day.

Elise sniffled and blindly reached into her satchel for a tissue. She couldn't even drive downtown and park because what she had left in the bank had been shelled out to pay mortgage, a few groceries, and get a train pass to carry her through the month. She didn't complain because at some point, she'd catch her breath and a break—both at the same time.

Fighting for the life of her sister was something Elise would never regret. But the aftermath to her finances and the never-ending strain between her and the family was putting her closer to the edge of emotional bankruptcy.

A tap on the window startled her.

Elise absently patted her tears away with the tissue.

"Ma'am, is everything all right?" Officer Montgomery questioned.

She rolled down the window. "Your kindness was the nicest thing that's happened to me in a long time." She looked up toward the empty bridge. "Thank you. But the next train comes in two hours. By then, the agency will call someone else to take the spot I was going for."

The officer scanned the area. Only a few cars zipped by them.

"Traffic isn't bad right now. You could make it downtown in about thirty minutes and still get there on time."

"I could but …" Elise hesitated then abruptly added, "I can' t …" She couldn't voice the words—she had everything, down to the last penny budgeted—and parking downtown was an arm, a leg and a couple of someone else's toes.

Officer Montgomery placed a hand over hers. "I'm really sorry."

His touch was wonderful. She centered her self-control with a quickness. "What's done is done. Recently my life has been hit with more curve balls than a dodge ball tournament. So I'm going home to regroup. I'll be fine." Her voice wavered on the last sentence, but she took a deep breath, tossed her hair over her shoulder, and held her head high. Seconds later, she turned the key in the ignition to start the car. "Take care."

Officer Montgomery reached for her hand again. "No, you're not," he ordered. "You will park your car in that lot just ahead. Then you'll get into my car, and I'll get you to work on time." He stepped back and finished, "That's what you're going to do."

She looked at him, her tears blurring her vision. "That's what I'm going to do?"

He nodded.

Elise took a moment before whispering, "All right, then."

Officer Montgomery headed for his squad car again and added, "I'll be right behind you."

This time, she did smile ... a little.

CHAPTER 2

*W*hen Elise slipped into the passenger seat of the cruiser, he pointed to the seat belt and waited until she strapped in before he closed her door. As soon as he called the station to inform them that he would be back on shift in an hour, they were off.

"What are you thinking right now?" he asked as he sped onto the expressway.

"I'm thinking that my day may have started off terribly, but things are definitely looking up. Thank you so much for this." She grinned over at him. "And I'm sorry for falling apart on you like that."

He laughed and said, "We all go through rough times."

"Do yours make you look like a blubbering idiot?"

Officer Montgomery shrugged. "Weeeeeell, not exactly."

"Like I said, I've been going through a rough patch," she said, relishing his laughter.

The man was absolutely sexy, with a dash of bad-boy swagger thrown in for good measure. He was a definite change from the type of man she normally went for. Officer Montgomery, despite everything she was going through had managed to do the impossible—

excite her. Something Elise thought Cecil, her ex-husband, had ruined for her.

Cecil Payne had shattered her desire for corporate men. After their disappointing marriage there was nothing appealing about the corporate executive over-moneyed entitled types that she even wanted to think about. They were not married a full year before he laid down an entirely new set of demands. A stay at home wife, preferably in the kitchen and bedroom, and not precisely in that order. She would never have signed up for the long program if that was the case. To this day, she couldn't understand how he had managed to be so good at keeping his true intentions hidden.

Cecil found more issues with her as their marriage grew older. Elise saw a selfish side of him that rivered chills down her spine. He disapproved of her working outside of the home—said it reflected badly on a man of his success. She would often argue, "I bet Jay-Z doesn't have a problem with Beyoncé bringing home the bacon." For which he would glare at her and turn cold.

Elise knew she was not built to just be trophy wife. It was not in her nature. She had dreams, too. To fuel those, and appease her overbearing spouse, she started an extremely successful home-based business in graphic design. She had the best of both worlds until Elena, her twin, became ill and then every aspect of her world fell apart.

"I've been so swallowed up with trying to get my life back on track," she said, "I feel guilty when I forget to take the time to be grateful for being alive, for being healthy." She kept her focus on a hooptie with an obvious alignment issue ahead of them. "Some people haven't been this blessed."

He nodded, maneuvering the cruiser into the fast lane.

"When you pulled me over," she said, "I wasn't thinking what I'd done wrong, only what it was going to cost me. And lately, my 'cost me' list is longer than Beyoncé's good weave."

"I can understand that," he said softly. "But it doesn't have to stay that way. You have to take one bite of the elephant at a time."

"You know, I never cared for lines like that," she countered, giving him a wary glance. "Who eats an elephant anyway?"

7

He chuckled and gave her the side eye.

"True. Allow me to re-phrase it. You can only drink a glass of water one sip, one gulp, at a time."

Elisa crossed her arms. "That's just as bad as having your cake and eating it too," she said dryly. "I mean, why have a cake if you can't eat it?"

Officer Montgomery shook his head. "You have to see things in a more positive light, Ms. Payne."

"How can you say that?" she asked. "Especially in your line of work."

He was silent a few moments, then, "I choose to be optimistic." He glanced at her for a brief moment before putting his focus back on the road. "For instance, I chose to believe the best about you, so when I checked your record and found it clean, I decided not to issue those tickets."

Elise looked at the clock, the odometer, and then back at him.

He looked over at her and gave her a toothy grin. "I'm not turning that siren on."

"It doesn't automatically come on if you're going over the speed limit?"

Officer Montgomery roared with laughter. "No, Ms. Payne, it doesn't."

"Elise."

"I'm Roman, but I'll admit I kind of like the way you say, Officer Montgomery." He cast a glance in her direction. "It sounds ... encouraging?"

She gave him a low, throaty chuckle. "Well, I don't think you want to know what I was calling you before I read your name tag."

"Oh, I can imagine."

They drove in silence for a while as she watched him concentrate on maneuvering the post-rush-hour traffic.

"Can you get into trouble for this?" she whispered, coming to a sudden realization.

"I won't tell if you won't," he winked.

She zippered her lips and tossed away an imaginary key.

The action had them both laughing.

* * *

FIFTEEN MINUTES LATER, Roman pulled in front of a silver and glass structure that stretched for half a block on LaSalle Street in front of the murky waters of the Chicago River. He stepped out and helped her to the sidewalk. She stood on tiptoe and pressed a kiss to his cheek.

He smiled, then narrowed his gaze on her. "Now, the next time I catch you speeding, I'm giving you that ticket, young lady."

"The next time you see me, I'll be able to *afford* that ticket ... Officer Montgomery."

Roman's smile was something that angels could sing about all day long. The woman who ended up with him would be getting the entire package—gentleman, witty, sexy, strong, and sensuous. Oh, and single —no ring on his finger. Why couldn't she land *those* types of men?

"And if you ever need anything—even just to talk—please don't hesitate to call," he said, holding out a business card.

Elise slipped it from between his fingers. Their hands touched briefly, and that sliver of excitement vibrated between them again. She quickly tucked the card inside her satchel. "I'll only call with good news."

"In my line of work, I could use it sometimes."

Elise pressed a kiss to his cheek, then stepped around him and couldn't help the saucy little strut that took her to the revolving door.

"Things will work out for you. Trust me," he called out as her hand touched the glass.

She gave him one last smile over her shoulder. "I'm going to hold you to that, Officer Montgomery."

CHAPTER 3

O fficer Roman Montgomery merged back onto the expressway, unable to get Elise Payne out of his mind. He was thrown by the abrupt beauty in her defiant will to rein in her tears. When she pushed up her chin and tossed her silky mane of dark hair, he wanted to pull her out of the car and kiss her. Such courage and perseverance in that small gesture.

She was in pain. Her eyes said it more than her words ever could. Even her humor couldn't hide it. She had been through something hard and rough and although she was battered, down, and sullen she was still determined to make it at all costs. He could admire that in any woman. He could admire that in *his* woman.

What had caused such staunch pain in her? A man in her life? No, that couldn't be it, not with the way she had laid that kiss on him. It was soft, inviting, sensuous—a thank you, but ... damn. He had witnessed her transformation from a woman who had been ready to retreat to a woman who was very aware of herself. The pain had taken a back seat for just a moment. He was grateful that he was there to see it—and hoped to be around to see it again.

Roman was no stranger to pain himself. His wife of eight years had been taken much too soon—the cancer that had ripped through her body had been as unexpected as Roman's unanswered prayers. And then she faded away, leaving only memories and an empty hole in his heart where love should have resided.

Only recently had the loneliness that had settled into his soul begun to lift. Ever since his wife died, he had been awakened by dreams in which she encouraged him to let her go and move on. He had ignored her so many times, but seeing Elise made something within his heart quicken.

The heavy warmth of arousal below his belt was also trying to have its say on the matter. He wanted that woman! Every ounce of professional decorum said that it couldn't happen. He had helped her today because he felt that it was the right thing to do, not because he wanted something in return.

Roman couldn't pinpoint why he'd made the decision to take her into The Loop, but the fact that she was doing something to change her circumstances was a definite plus, and he was glad to play a small part in it.

Lately, officers nationwide were being called on the carpet for offering favors to female motorists who broke the law in exchange for a vertical tango. More than anything, he was a major proponent of staying on the right side of professional ethics. Elise stirred an urge in him, something that over-ruled his ethics, and as much as he enjoyed his paycheck, seeing her so vulnerable was something he could not allow.

It was gut instinct not to ticket her, and rather a sudden remembrance of his oath—to protect *and* serve. His mind understood that, his morals understood that, too, but something about that woman called to him and he knew it would be a long time before he would get that encounter out of his mind.

One thing was for sure, Roman could never see Elise Payne again. Her combination of beauty, strength, humor, and sexiness was more dangerous than a bullet straight to the heart.

* * *

ELISE, get your mind in the game, young lady, and off of that sexy beast of man. No time for distractions.

She chanted that mantra all the way up on the elevator.

When security escorted her through the series of glass doors and into the reception area on the 37th floor, a perky red-haired woman was waiting. "I'm Theresa. Ms. Bernatz would like to see you."

Elise paused mid-step. "Isn't that the human resources manager?"

"Yes," Theresa said and started down the hall.

Elise hesitantly followed. "But I'm supposed to meet with Ms. Hippen to start a temp position."

"That's changed." Theresa halted, stashed a stack of manila folders in a cabinet to the right of the desk and picked up the pace again. "Right this way, please."

Elise's heart fluttered with apprehension. She followed the slender woman past a row of offices that all had the same bright white walls, gray shades, and silver fixtures—absolutely no color whatsoever.

Things will work out for you. Trust me.

Theresa rapped her pale knuckles against a frosted glass door and got a, "Come in."

Elise was directed to take the chair across from a bottled blonde with a dour expression and hair pinned in a bun so tight that fresh air would have paid money to get to her scalp.

Several ticks of time passed before Ms. Bernatz looked up and gave Elise a thorough once-over, taking in the classic navy power suit, lavender blouse, pearl earrings and necklace. Finally, she said, "I don't think you'll be right for the position."

Elise fought to smother her disappointment. To cope, she reminded herself that she had shown up on time and would at least be guaranteed four hours of work per the temp agency contract. That was a blessing. She would spend the rest of the day assessing the hours needed to re-launch her graphic design business and move forward with her life. That was a blessing, too.

Things will work out for you. Trust me, echoed through her again.

Elise exhaled a deep breath, lifted her head, looked directly at Ms. Bernatz and said, "I understand. Thank you for considering me."

She stood and the woman's brow furrowed. "Where are you going, Ms. Payne?"

"Home," Elise replied. "You said I wasn't right for the position."

The woman's thin pink lips spread into something that was neither smile nor frown. "Sit down."

Elise complied.

"The temp-to-perm position we called you in for, yes you're not the right fit."

Ms. Bernatz removed her rimmed glasses, cleaned them and put them back on. She flipped open a thick manila folder and added, "This file is for the managing partners you worked with a few months ago."

Elise's eyes bulged. The file was almost three inches deep.

"Yes," Ms. Bernatz smirked. "I can tell by the look on your face you remember them."

Elise flashed back to three months earlier. She had enjoyed assisting the four of them with a national case that was still in the headlines. But more than that, they had treated her as if she was a member of a team, not a lowly assistant. That counted for a lot in her book.

"Anyway, thirty minutes ago their current assistant tendered her resignation. She's moving to Phoenix with her husband," Ms. Bernatz said sourly. "Mr. Esbrook, Ms. Riff. Ms. Bucci, and Mr. Burrichter asked—hell, practically demanded—that we find out if you could fill the position. Permanently. Effective now."

Elise gripped the edges of the chair and tried to not to scream for joy.

"The position starts at ..." Ms. Bernatz passed over a new hire package, and the salary almost made Elise's jaw drop. "We have excellent medical and insurance benefits that begin the day you do, seventy hours vacation the first year, seventy hours of personal/sick time, all major holidays, and one floating holiday to use as you see fit. Will this be acceptable to you?"

Things will work out for you. Trust me.

Elise closed her eyes, and Roman's image swam into focus. She opened them to find that Ms. Bernatz was looking at her with an obvious impatient expression.

Elise licked pursed her lips trying to pull it together. "When do you want me to start?"

That woman brightened with just those few words. "Support Services is handling the workload and filing today. You can start with a fresh desk tomorrow."

"Sounds like a plan," Elise said as she began filling out the paperwork.

Ms. Bernatz took the sheets as each one was completed. "You'll be put on our payroll today, and I'll see to it that you get a paycheck this Friday." Ms. Bernatz extended her hand. "I'll see you bright and early in the morning. Enjoy the rest of your day, Ms. Payne and welcome to Esbrook, Riff, Burrichter & Bucci."

"Thank you so much."

Elise left the building with a lot more pep in her step. She owed Officer Montgomery more than a simple thank you. She was going to send that man something that would curl his toes and put a smile on those sexy lips of his.

CHAPTER 4

With a smile wide enough to turn corners before the rest of her, Elise boarded the METRA to travel to the lot where her car was parked. Grateful she had the fare to make the trek back to where her rollercoaster journey started a few hours ago. All courtesy of the handsome Officer Roman Montgomery's earlier transport to her downtown destination. His compassion allowed her to have one of her prayers answered, becoming a full-time employee.

Nestled in her seat, Elise briefly closed her eyes. She silently planned what she was going to do to express her thankfulness for Roman's kindness. A soft moan escaped her lips as a vivid image of his sexy, uniformed stature entered her thoughts. Coughing from the burly man seated a few feet away and the sound of ringing snatched Elise out of that pleasurable moment. Her eyes shot open, and she looked at the screen. She was excited to share her good news with the caller.

"Hi, Milan. How are you?" she asked and couldn't keep the cheerful sound from her voice.

"Hey, E. I'm doing good," her friend replied. "You sound like you just hit the jackpot."

"I did," she squealed. "Guess what, Sis?"

Chuckling, Milan said, "You found a man."

"Maybe I did," Elise replied, a little deflated that she'd already figured it out. "Anyway, the actual news is that I have a permanent job as an assistant to the managing partners who I did the temp work for a few months ago."

"See, I told you everything would be all right. I'm so happy for you."

Elise had been friends with Milan for over ten years. She met the five-foot-six-inch, bronze, curvaceous powerhouse at the library while in junior high school and formed a tight-knit bond. Having a shared interest in learning and expanding their knowledge beyond the area they lived in. The two women became a strong support system for one another.

Growing up in Chicago, they both had tough home lives due to conflict with family members. In spite of that, both women were successful in their chosen fields. While Elise was a highly successful entrepreneur, Milan dedicated her life to social work at a local community center that involved the protection of women and children from unhealthy relationships.

"Thank you, Sis." Elise paused and the image of Roman came to mind. "There is something else."

"Hmm, and what's that?" Milan asked, with the sound of the copier churning on the other end.

Scanning the area to make sure no one was eavesdropping, she said, "I met this fine ass police officer. Girl, I mean he is a walking wet dream."

"Well, damn. Where did you find him in this vast wasteland of crazy men?"

"I was *kind of* speeding and he pulled me over."

"There is no such thing as *kind of* speeding," Milan shot back "Just own it, you wanna' be NASCAR driver."

Laughing, Elise shook her head because Milan had a lot of nerve. She was a lead foot too. "Whatever. He was a very nice gentleman."

"Don't forget sexy," her long-time friend said.

"Giiiiiirrlll ... anyway," she said, thinking that sexy wasn't even the word. "I have to go. I'll chat with you later."

Thirty minutes later, she was stepping off the platform in Hegewisch and practically skipping to her car. Once Elise was strapped into her seatbelt, she turned on the radio to the velvet tenor sounds of Luther Vandross singing "Lovely Day." Watching her speed, she took a detour to the supermarket down the street from her house to pick up the select items needed for the special dish that she was cooking for Officer Montgomery.

Placing her groceries on the kitchen island, she grabbed the cell phone out of her black Coach purse to check on her missed call. Not recognizing the number, she hit the voicemail button.

"I've been trying to reach you. Where the hell are you?" the irritating voice rasped on the other end.

Rolling her eyes, she moved the phone away from her ear and took a slow, deep breath. Wanting to make sure that everything was all right, she reluctantly called the number.

"Why has it taken you this long to call me back?" No greeting or kind tone.

"First, I don't answer to you anymore," she shot back in the calmest voice she could manage. "Is Jordan all right?"

"He's doing just fine, and you would know that if you answered the damn phone when I call."

"If there is nothing wrong with our son, then this phone call is unnecessary."

"You listen to me ..." he roared.

Click

Placing the phone down on the counter, Elise closed her eyes for a few seconds. Any conversation she had with that man was exhausting. His controlling nature was not something she wished to tolerate. It was just a matter of time before she had her son back in her home and then communication would be very limited with her ex. For far too long her ex held all the power.

"How the hell did I ever get mixed up with that fool?" she said to herself while looking up at the ceiling. "God, give me the strength to endure as I work to get my baby boy back home with me."

After prepping the delicious surprise for her knight, who saved the day, she showered and changed into a rose-colored silk lounge set. Elise walked into the living room and took a seat on the black and grey contemporary suede sofa centered in the spacious area. A matching loveseat and chaise surrounded it. Turning on the wall mounted, 60-inch television, a syndication of the crime drama series Miami Vice appeared on the screen. Roman's face appeared in an instant.

The man was an Adonis compared to the man that she allowed herself to fall in love with previously. Now, Elise was divorced and planning to get her son back from one of the most challenging human beings who walked the earth. Picking up the glass of Prosecco from the grey end table, she took a sip and focused on thinking about the positive parts of the day. She wouldn't allow Cecil the pleasure of ruining that for her.

Tomorrow, she'd begin strategizing her next moves as well as brightening up a certain police officer's day.

CHAPTER 5

"Yo, Monty. Package for ya."

Roman frowned at Ken Amorio, who had an annoying habit of shortening his last name to Monty. To him, Monty sounded more like some old man with a lisp, a bad comb-over, and a mouth that would put a sailor to shame.

Roman sauntered toward the front of the station, past the cubicles at the end of the winding hall until he made it to the intake counter. Several of his fellow officers had gathered around the bright white box, which was tied with a purple bow and had a card wedged on top.

Ken his partner, who had a wicked sense of humor and an even greater flair for creativity, slid the box toward Roman, who immediately plucked the card nestled under the bow.

"She was very specific about making sure we didn't tip it to one side or the other," Ken said, stroking his goatee.

"She?" Roman asked.

Ken's mouth widened in a sly smile. "Sweet little piece of thick honey candy. Curves that could turn corners before the rest of her."

"Who'd you piss off?" asked Annette, a petite, mocha woman sporting a short cap of dark curls with the barest hint of silver. She stood on tip-toe, trying to get a better peek at the box. "Think it's a bomb?" With a hand sliding up her hip, she glared in Ken's direction. "Should I call the squad?"

Roman prepared to tear open the flap on the lavender envelope. "It's not a bomb."

"Don't know why she'd be looking for you." Inez clapped a hand over Roman's shoulder, her locks shifting forward with that small movement. "You're still looking for Mrs. Right when I keep telling you you'd be better off looking for Miss Right Now."

Actually, her definition only had one description—Ms. Inez herself. Roman had been fending her off since she joined the force. Workplace romances almost never ended well and he couldn't afford to have anyone hesitate to have his back if he was in a dangerous situation.

Suddenly the group—all three of them—inched in. Annette, Ken, and Inez all had their focus on that white box as though Christmas had arrived and Santa had passed them over. But they were willing to share any gifts that Old St. Nick had bestowed upon Roman.

Roman presented his back to his nosy brethren. When he saw the evenly-spaced script on the inside, he grinned.

I got the position!! They hired me for a different full time position!
Thank you.
Thank you.
THANK YOU!
Elise Payne
P.S. This is my favorite pan. Please make sure it finds its way back home
- 312-555-6512.

Roman's smile widened. Ken, taller than Roman by a couple of inches, peered over his shoulder, trying to get a better look. The distraction worked.

Annette managed to slide in and get an eyeful before Roman could snatch the card away. "It's a woman, y'all," she crowed in a fake Southern accent. "Betcha there's some vittles in that thar box."

Chuckles sounded all around him.

Ken, who was known for his hearty appetite, rubbed his hands together. "Well, they say that the way to a man's heart is through his stomach."

"Actually, it's through his mama," Annette corrected, waggling her ring finger at everyone. "Ask me how I know."

Ken leaned forward and gave her a kiss, which caused a few grumbles from the rest of the crew and cries of, "Get a room."

"So open it already," Inez demanded.

Roman pulled up the first flap. The scent of nutmeg and cinnamon wafted up to him, and his stomach did a cartwheel of joy. He lifted the final flap, and the *oohs* and *ahhhs* that echoed around him matched his sentiments exactly. Evidently, Elise knew exactly how to get his attention.

What lay before him was a masterpiece of peach cobbler. Perfectly layered lattice crust, juices trying to make a mad dash for the sides, golden peaches that looked ready to make a quantum leap into his mouth and swim for the borders of his taste buds.

Roman reached for the silver fork that she was thoughtful enough to put in with everything else. He felt more like lifting that utensil and directing some unseen angelic orchestra. Time stood still. He scooped out that first forkful and suddenly remembered he had an audience.

He scanned the area to find that several more co-workers had come over. Each and every one of them was watching him intently. He should have waited until he was back at his desk to unveil his prize. But it was too late to turn back now. He placed that first forkful on the tip of his tongue before sliding it all the way into his mouth and tasting ... heaven.

"Oooo, I know that look," Ken offered. He turned to the others. "That right there is the look of a man who's tasting something even better than good sex." He slapped Roman on the back. "Am I right?"

Roman could barely speak. "Ohhh, yes," he moaned.

Roman closed his eyes and let the flavors make love to his tongue as the image of the woman who prepared such a delectable dessert came to mind. That one taste was like having Elise Payne on a platter. The sweetness, the buttery, flaky layers, the—

"I call cobbs."

NALEIGHNA KAI & U. M. HIRAM

Roman's eyes flew open and narrowed on Annette. "Back off, short stack. This right here is a solo adventure," he proclaimed.

He quickly packed up his treasure and put as much distance between himself and the expectant crowd as he could.

"Be like that," Ken snapped, right on his heels. "Weren't you the one begging me to teach you how to Step?"

"Yep."

"Didn't I help you out?"

Roman didn't miss a beat. "Yep."

"So what's the problem?"

"No problem," Roman shot back. "You taught me how to Step; I taught you how to Salsa. A fair exchange ain't no robbery."

Ken shook his head, frowning. "I thought I was your boy. I can't get some of that cobbler, man?"

"Nope," Roman slid into his chair before taking in another forkful.

"Aw come on, man," Inez whined, moving to stand next to Ken. "Give up the good stuff."

"Not happening," Roman shot back, smacking his lips happily. "Mine—all mine."

"That smells good, too." Annette licked her lips, and for a moment Ken wasn't focusing on peach cobbler anymore. His eyes roamed the petite curves of the unit's sharp-shooter. That brother looked ready to spread his wife on the desk and have *her* for dessert.

Their gazes locked, Ken's eyebrow went up. Annette nodded toward the utility closet.

Another bite made it into Roman's mouth as he said, "Go away people. No means, no."

Roman looked up to see the newlyweds vanish quicker than he could take another bite.

Captain Austin appeared at Roman's desk. Everyone made a hasty exit to their respective places and suddenly pretended like they had some work to do. The Captain scanned the area, making sure the coast was clear before he presented an empty saucer and his own fork.

Roman gathered his box to his chest like a wounded bird. "Sorry, Captain. This was a special delivery. A *personal* delivery."

STOP IN THE NAME OF LOVE

"Does it have anything to do with your little off-the-clock excursion and those extra thirty-two miles on your cruiser yesterday?" the Captain asked with a wink. "Was that a *personal* delivery in *company property?*"

Suddenly the box was at the end of the desk, all flaps open again. "Gee, Captain, would you like some peach cobbler?" Roman flashed an exaggerated grin.

"Damn skippy," he answered, sliding Roman a clean fork. "And take it from the side you *didn't* dip in." Captain Austin gestured to the treat and said, "She must be something special."

Roman scanned the box, the contents, the ribbon, the care that went into the presentation, which was a good representation of the woman he barely knew. "Yes, she is. But it can't go anywhere. You know the policy and—"

"I don't see any problem with you calling her to say thank you," the Captain said around a forkful of food. He closed his eyes to savor the moment, causing Roman to growl, "I'll get on that ... right after you get your paws out of my cobbler."

Captain Austin chuckled all the way to his office, ignoring the envious looks everyone threw his way.

Roman quickly repackaged his gift and stared at the phone for a few moments. Internal Affairs were stringent about the types of gifts they could receive and any questionable interaction with the public. Chicago police were coming under fire in a major way, but his unit and the entire department had stayed clear of things—not even flouting the boundaries at any given time. He glanced at the cobbler, and it brought to mind the first day that he arrived at his foster parents home.

The brown-skinned woman, with a houseful of children from every ethnic background, made him feel welcome by taking him into the kitchen, sliding a hot meal in front of him, then explaining that no matter where he'd been and what he'd been through, he was now in a place she'd love for him to call home. The laughter of the other children echoed around him, which was a far cry from what he'd experienced in other places. But it was when she placed a hand over his, and said, "You're going to be all right. If *you* choose to be all right. Life might have taken you here and there, but here, you'll learn how to choose what you want in life and go after it."

She followed the meal and that wonderful declaration by sharing a healthy portion of peach cobbler with him, while telling him stories that brought on the first real laughter he'd had in months and set his heart at ease. Mama Joyce was right about so many other things. And he, a Latino born on the east side of Chicago, was grateful for her loving touch and pure heart.

Elise was just as warm as that wonderful woman who had thrown him, and all of his multi-ethnic brothers and sisters, a life-line. Even with Elise's teary eyes, her heart-shaped face, sensual cheek bones, generous mouth, almond-shaped eyes, and honey skin had Roman wanting to know if she was beautiful all over. But the complex mixture of vulnerability and strength was the most compelling thing about her—as if she held the weight of the world on her shoulders but still had to put on a brave face.

I don't see any problem with you calling her to say thank you.

Roman snatched the phone from the cradle and felt a thrum of pleasure whip through him when she answered on the second ring.

"Hey, Officer Montgomery."

"Hey yourself, Ms. Payne. I hear congratulations are in order."

"Yes," Elise cheered. "I am now a *permanent* legal secretary."

"That's awesome," he crowed. "And speaking of awesome." He flaked off a piece of the crust and popped it into his mouth. "This peach cobbler is a beautiful thing."

"I'm glad you like it," she said with a throaty chuckle. "I was going to send a whole meal, but I didn't think you'd be interest—"

"What did you cook?" he said, snapping his attention away from the dessert.

She rattled off the contents of a soul food dinner, and his stomach instantly said, *You'd better get some of that too.* But his mind said, *no, you shouldn't. Just thank her and be done.*

"I get off in thirty minutes," he said ignoring his mental filters. "Too late to swing by?"

"Not at all," she replied. "Did you want a plate to go, or would you prefer to dine in?"

All thoughts of keeping things strictly professional went for a long walk on a short pier. The woman had soul food—a home cooked meal waiting on the stove. Roman was about to come in for an emergency landing. And he would see her one last time.

"I'd like to have dinner with you, if that's not too much trouble."

"No trouble at all." He could *feel* her smile through the phone. "I'll be waiting for you."

CHAPTER 6

The man was coming to dinner. *Dinner!*

Elise placed the phone on the cradle and tried to get her heart rate back to a normal pace. She put a low fire under three of the pots, slid two pans in the oven, and did a quick sweep of the area, and quickly organized the paperwork scattered over the kitchen table.

When she arrived home the previous day, she had pulled out her business plan, list of former contacts, a marketing plan and went to work. Six hours later, she had a plan of attack for making sure she would get to a place again where doing something she loved would bring her enough financial security that she would not need to work for anyone else.

Then she pulled things together to make that peach cobbler, praying that Roman was the type of man who loved it as much as she did. Well, it must have hit the spot. The last time she had a man willingly in her home or in her bed was … well, Moses had been bringing down those tablets with the Ten Commandments.

Elise ran back down the stairs and removed the papers she had on the dining room table—all the evidence of the hard work she had put in trying to get her personal and business affairs in order. The day before, none of her creditors or former clients had wanted to work with her.

While she was caring for her twin sister, Cecil took that opportunity to dismantle her entire life, her hard won success, and her family loyalty all because *he* felt neglected. Cecil committed sabotage at every turn. He ripped through her bank accounts—both business and private, then shut down her company's website, purposely neglected to pay bills, shut off her business phone lines.

Once Elise realized what he had done, she confronted him. Then Cecil got mean—real mean—physically abusive mean. To add insult to injury, he was causing her even more trouble now all because she had the nerve to leave him the first time his fists had landed her in the hospital.

Elise had left with just her son and the clothes on their backs. After that, everything that could hit the fan—did. And Elise was still covered in a great deal of it. Getting this position would mean a new beginning, a chance to make things better, and a way to get her life back before she made the mistake of marrying the wrong man.

Now, with a few strategic phone calls, not only was she poised to be back in the personal finances saddle, but her former clients were willing to give her the second chance that her ex-husband never wanted her to have. The rest, she'd tackle much later. Right now, she had more pressing business at hand.

Dinner with Officer Roman Montgomery. The golden Adonis.

Elise tore up the stairs, aiming to trade her pajamas for an outfit that was more "come hither" but not quite "come and get it."

She was putting the final touches on the dining room table when the doorbell rang. Her heart dropped into her belly. She jetted to the full length mirror and sized up her appearance. Elise had settled for a simple red dress, classic black pumps, silver earrings and a necklace to match. To that she added a light dusting of make-up and a dash of Celebrate perfume in all the right places.

Elise opened the door to find Officer Montgomery holding a purple Cymbidium orchid plant. "This is beautiful," she said softly, then locked in on her white box in his other hand. "You couldn't leave that at work?"

"And be thrown in jail tomorrow if it came up missing?"

She laughed, stepping aside to allow him inside and only then did she see that he had another box as well.

"My captain already blackmailed me for a slice."

"Blackmail?" She frowned up at him, gesturing for him to follow her toward the dining room. "Isn't that like … illegal?"

"You're asking me or telling me?" His gaze swept across her—head to toe—and appreciation lit within those dark brown eyes. "You look absolutely beautiful."

"Well, you don't look so bad yourself."

"Must be the uniform," he said, giving her the cobbler to set on the counter as he removed his protective vest and gun holster and set them on top of the fridge.

She set the plant on the kitchen table and said, "Uniforms don't impress me one way or the other." Elisa gave him a flirty smile. "But the man wearing it…" She left the comment hanging in the air between them and turned toward the plant. "I'm going to take this to work. It'll brighten up my desk."

Roman held out the other box to her and the twinkle in his eyes almost made her afraid to open.

He washed his hands at the sink, taking a sweeping look at her kitchen. "Your place is nice."

"Thank you," she smiled over to him again and flipped open the top to find a black derby inside—actually two of them. She clamped down on what she had to stay because the emotions that came forth at his thoughtfulness, made it nearly impossible to speak. "You remembered."

"Yes, and it might not be the ones you had, but I hope it will still bring a smile to face when you remember her."

A few seconds passed and she went to him and put her arms around him. "Thank you so much for this. You don't know how much this means to me."

Moments later, they fixed their plates, and he held out her chair.

Once he was settled across from her he asked, "How was your first day at work?"

Elise couldn't help the elation that soared through her. "Awesome. I couldn't have picked a better position if I tried," she said. "The partner has a very busy schedule—he's a traveler. But the associates— a blonde workaholic, a night owl with organization issues, and a fresh out of law school rookie—are die-hard work horses, but they've been real cool about how they want things done."

Roman nodded his attention to the conversation but did not miss a beat in getting his eat on. Elise almost wanted to laugh at how he looked at his food like he had just won the lottery and was staring at the winning numbers.

She enjoyed her meal, not missing something about Roman. He ate in the opposite way that she did. Elise liked eating one entrée at a time. All the greens, then onto finishing off her mac and cheese and so forth. Not Roman. His appetite called for the full taste bud experience. He stabbed his greens, mac and cheese then his potato salad and savored all of it at once. It was kind of sexy.

Roman commanded all her attention when he took a bite of her fried chicken.

Is he purring?

"I thought your peach cobbler was euphoric, but this right here …" He shook his head and wiped his mouth with a napkin. "Woman, are you trying to make me fall in love with you?"

"If I could do that with a single meal, then you were an easy target from the word go."

Roman roared with laughter. "Touché."

"I'm glad you like it," she said, giving him a wide smile. "Maybe when I fix Italian or Mexican, you can lose your mind, but I think we'll be all right on this one."

"Maybe," he said, and at that moment their gazes locked. The music flowed from old school R&B tunes to the Emilio Estefan remix of Lenny Kravitz's *Tell Me Mama*. "Do you Salsa?" he asked, surprised by the choice of music.

"I do enough to get by," Elise confirmed taking another forkful of food to her mouth.

Roman stood so fast, she blinked. His hand extended. "Shall we?"

"I take it that you know what you're doing," Elise wiped her lips and rose from the table.

"I do enough to get by," he tossed back with a wink.

Roman guided her flawlessly to the living room and then she was in his arms.

"I shouldn't be doing this with you," she whispered.

His lifted eyebrow said it all: I'm in control, and I say you are doing this with me.

"Roman?"

"Trust me," he crooned.

After that, the best she could manage was to try like hell to keep up. She did lose her way a few times, but he would put her in a basic right turn to get her back on point or pause a split second, whisper a count, and whip her back into action as though she hadn't broken their stride.

The man was one hell of a dancer. But even more than that, he was a great lead—which made their pairing that much better.

What would he be like in …

Oh, hell, no, she had *not* just thought that. Elise wanted to hide under her house. She felt her cheeks heating up.

No, no, no. Get these thoughts of this golden hunk of a man out of your head right now. No more thoughts of his delicious, hard body stretched out on your Egyptian cotton sheets. Stop it right now, young lady. Don't you dare imagine your arms wrapped around him as he parts your thighs—

Roman twirled her out and asked, "You all right? You look out of breath."

"Oh, yeah, great. Keep going. Keep going," she gasped, thankful that her exertion hid the real reason for her flushed features.

She swayed into him, the strength of him, the way his hands held on to hers, stroked her, was heady. All she could think about was how good it felt to be in this man's arms—the arms of a man she wanted.

Roman smelled wonderful, adding to the alluring seduction of his entire package. Elise would love to roam her hands across that well-toned body.

Then fear struck a chord. The attraction for this man was too strong, too fast, she had too much to accomplish before falling for anyone. She had to get away.

Before she could run off the floor, Roman snapped her back into a turn. Elise didn't get a chance to say a word before he gripped her hips, held firm, and said through his teeth, "Keep moving."

Shocked, she did. Her next set of dance moves were next to impossible to do with someone holding her so sensually, but her hips moved with him for several ticks of time before he spun her completely around with him—still entwined—and then back to a normal mode of Salsa dancing.

A shimmer of pleasure whipped through her. "Sweet Je-sus," she whispered.

"Yeah, something like that," he answered and pulled her back to him, the closeness becoming something she wanted, needed.

Ever since she had parted ways with Cecil, whenever Elise ventured out to dance, men knew there was a line they did not cross. It was in her body language. Yet her body language with Roman was screaming: *cross the line—please.*

She smiled at him and wanted to thank him. Twirling in his arms, the way he maneuvered her so effortlessly was proof that Cecil Payne had not stripped away her ability to be a woman—a sensuous woman. Something the weasel claimed she never was.

"Damn, you're good," she whispered to him.

He winked. "So I've been told."

"And no shortage of ego, either."

Roman roared with laughter and dipped her. They were so close she could feel his soul thumping with every beat of his heart, the heat of his passion with every pant of his breath.

Elise's lips parted of their own accord. Roman took full command of the innocent invitation and planted his smooth lips over hers. Her head tilted up, welcoming him into the silky depths of her world. His

31

tongue teased that opening, tasting, asking for permission that she was only too ready to give. Oh, how she wanted this kiss.

Her body and mind went into sensory overload. With one intense kiss, Roman had accomplished the impossible. She could not believe it. She wanted every pulse-pounding inch of him. She wanted him like her next breath.

Formality, proper etiquette, and her 'good girl' upbringing be damned. The way his hands stretched out across her lower back, then traveled to twist in her hair nearly melted her knees. They could have stayed that way for an eternity.

"Do you want to know the moment that I knew I wanted you?" he asked, ending the kiss and eternity too soon.

Elise had an idea of how she must appear to him—too dazed to answer.

She was right when he said, "When you struggled to hold back your tears."

CHAPTER 7

The look of absolute desire on Elise's face was about to get Roman in a boatload of trouble. No woman should look so wanton after being kissed and not be enjoyed to the fullest extent. His actions needed to be tempered with restraint for now. But if he had his way, when time and opportunity presented itself, nothing on this side of heaven would stop him from having Elise Payne.

Roman kept his Salsa moves sensual and distracting as he continued, "I could tell that there was so much going on with you. But your tears and that stiff upper lip bravado were what did it for me. There was something inspiring about you. Something strong, and sweet. Something I wanted to have, and not just for one night."

Roman pulled her to him, buried his head in the smooth curve of her shoulder and held her there for several moments.

"And on that note," he whispered. "I'm going to leave before I take this someplace we shouldn't go ..." his gaze narrowed on her as he added, "at least not tonight."

She nodded, and he put a few more inches of space between them.

"I'd like to take you out to dinner," he redirected.

"When," she asked.

NALEIGHNA KAI & U. M. HIRAM

He stroked a hand across her cheek. "Well, I'm on rotation for a stint at a half-way house the rest of this week, so next Friday."

Her face crinkled up, thinking. Roman had a feeling she was warring with responsibility and surrender.

Her answer confirmed it. "Upcoming projects."

"Friday after that?" Roman offered.

Elise grimaced.

He squinted his displeasure. "The Friday after that at seven."

She gulped. "All right."

He leveled a gaze at her. "Are you going to give me two syllable answers all night?"

"No."

Roman grinned. "Now we're down to one syllable."

"Friday after next at seven o'clock," she replied. "Dinner with you."

"That works for me," he said, giving her a warm smile. "See you then."

She walked him to the kitchen, where he retrieved his weapons and holstered them. "How should I dress?"

"Something to tease the hell out of me like you did tonight," he said. "Oh, and those heels you wore yesterday. I'm man enough to admit, you had my tongue hanging on my foot."

Elise couldn't help but smile. "You really know how to make a woman feel good."

"If that's all it takes, then you were an easy target from the word go."

"Touché," she said, making a funny face and he wanted to kiss her all over again.

"See you next week, but I'd like to call you before that."

"I'd like that." She grinned up at him and Roman realized he really needed to get out of this woman's house. Her sensual influence was fracturing his resolve.

He made it to the front door and did a one-eighty. "I forgot something."

"You don't trust it to stay here?" she protested sliding her hands on her soft hips.

34

"Nope. Hand over the peach cobbler, lady, and no one gets hurt," Roman commanded.

This time it was Elise's turn to laugh as she backtracked to retrieve his package.

Roman followed her and said at the kitchen's threshold, "And the rest of dinner too, please." He flashed a mischievous smile.

Elise presented both to him a few minutes later.

"I'm having this with breakfast, lunch, and dinner." Then he locked gazes with her and added, "And I'll think of you with every bite."

Roman smoothly juggled the containers in one hand and Elise in the other as he dropped a good night kiss on the woman so intense that food would be the last thing on either of their minds for a while.

CHAPTER 8

*T*hree days later, Elise was on her way to meet Milan for an overdue lunch date at Maggiano's Little Italy. They hadn't seen or talked to each other in a little while because of their busy schedules. She was ready to discuss Roman and the feelings that had been developing between them.

Elise entered the restaurant and was greeted by a smiling, petite hostess dressed in black slacks and an embroidered logo shirt. The delicious aromas of Italian food tickled her nostrils. Her stomach produced a light rumble as hints of basil, garlic, and rosemary filled the air.

"Welcome to Maggiano's," she said. "Are you dining in or picking up an order today?"

"I have a lunch reservation," Elise said.

"Great. May I please have your name?"

"Sure, it's Elise Payne, and the reservation should be for two.

"Yes ma'am, I have your reservation noted right here," the red-haired hostess said. "Would you like to be seated now or wait a few minutes for your guest to arrive?"

On cue, Milan entered the restaurant and gave her best friend a big hug. The hostess led them to their booth near a window facing the busy streets of downtown Chicago. A red and white tablecloth with a sheer white overlay covered the table. In the center was a lighted lavender and vanilla scented candle, while the cutlery was neatly arranged and glistened. As they waited for their server to come over, the ladies caught up about the events happening in their lives.

"E, it is so good to see you," Milan began. "I feel like it's been too long."

"I know, and I feel that same way," Elise said. "We need to do better about scheduling time more often."

"I agree. Now, tell me all about Mr. Roman Montgomery."

Laughing, Elise said, "Well damn. You are straight to the point, as always."

Winking and smiling, Milan said, "And you wouldn't want me any other way."

At that moment, a tall, handsome server with cropped black hair and mesmerizing blue eyes showed up at the table to take their drink orders. Both ladies already knew what they wanted to eat. Stuffed mushrooms were the choice of appetizer. Elise decided on the Chicken Parmesan for her entrée, while Milan chose Shrimp Scampi. The choice of drinks was tea and water since they both had to go back to work.

After taking a drink of her water and placing the glass down on the table, Elise told Milan about the dessert that she made for Roman, which led to his visit for an impromptu dinner and salsa dance at her house. Every time she thought about their bodies moving in rhythm and the eventual kisses, it made her want to move things along faster. That Adonis of a man made her body want to do the horizontal tango with him.

"Are you ready to take the next step with him this soon?"

"Yes," Elise answered, without hesitation. "He is such a kind and generous soul."

"And don't forget sexy," Milan said.

"Of course, but it's more than that with him."

Placing the fork on her plate, the woman sitting across from her looked as if she was contemplating her next words. "So, what makes this different from how you felt about Cecil?"

There it was, the elephant in the room that was filling up every nook and cranny. Elise anticipated Milan would question her because of all that she'd been through with that man.

"First, Roman is nothing like my ex-husband," she said. "I realize how fast things went with Cecil and ended up with me being married to a chauvinistic, controlling man. Something just feels different and right about this."

A few seconds of silence filled the space between them.

"If you are sure, then I have your back 100% of the way," Milan said. "Just know that should Roman get out of line, then he will be dealt with."

"Don't say that out loud, girl. He is a police officer."

Raising an eyebrow, her longtime friend said, "I don't care who he is. Mr. Montgomery aka Officer Friendly will catch this smoke if he shows his ass."

Elise looked at Milan and shook her head. "Duly Noted."

Moving the conversation away from her and Roman, she prompted Milan to share what had been going on in her life. Ranging from community work, family, and social life. As much as Elise knew the amazing person sitting on the other side of the table was rooting for her, she was praying for love to find its way back into Milan's. They both deserved a happily ever after.

* * *

ONE AND A HALF HOUR LATER, Elise was back in her office and working through the rest of the day. She had a great lunch with one of her best friends and looked forward to talking to Roman tonight. Weeks had been rolling by and it felt as if they had known each other for years.

The office phone interrupted Elise's concentration on her current projects. She had two top priority projects that her focus was on, one of which was due this afternoon. Shifting focus for a moment, she picked up without looking at the caller ID and her body reacted to the deep timbre that greeted her.

"Hello, Ms. Payne," Roman said. "How are you doing, beautiful?"

"Hi, Mr. Montgomery, this is an unexpected surprise."

"I couldn't wait to hear your voice, so I took a chance and called."

"I'm glad that you did, handsome," Elise said.

"How was your lunch date with Milan?"

"It was great. I'm glad I got to spend a little time with her today."

"I'm looking forward to meeting your bestie."

"Really, now? What makes you think that you'll be around that long to do so?"

With a mischievous tone to his voice, Roman said, "Sweetheart, I can guarantee you I will be around for a very long time."

Rendered speechless for a few seconds, Elise came back with a quirky response. "Well, I don't see how that's possible when you haven't *imprinted* on me."

"Mi Bella Elise, I'm not Jacob from Twilight," he began. "Trust me, when I do *imprint* on you, there's no turning back."

"That sounds like a challenge, and I look forward to rising to it."

"Just so we are clear, I will be the one rising to the challenge," he said, then lowered his voice. "You will be in for a mind-blowing, toe curling ride."

The couple talked for a few more minutes. After ending the call, Elise grabbed her chilled bottle of water and took a drink. Glancing at the clock, she gathered herself together and refocused on the task at hand. She would finish out the workday strong, then head home and take a cold shower. That man, oh that man.

CHAPTER 9

Two months later
        Saturday, 12:37 a.m.

Dinner at the Grand Lux Café on the Magnificent Mile, followed by a walk along Lake Michigan, had been a romantic interlude unlike any Elise had experienced with any other man. The kisses they shared were so raw and desperate that she was beginning to think she would have to carry an extra pair of underwear whenever she was with him.

Roman pulled up in front of Elise's ranch home, came around the front of his Audi, and opened the door for her.

"Would you like to come in for a cup of coffee?" she asked.

"Baby, the way I'm feeling right now," Roman answered, his voice husky with promise, "that wouldn't be the best move to make."

She looked up at him, frowning because she didn't get his meaning. The feelings between them were explosive. Because their schedules had sabotaged their original dinner date, they were forced to a realm of mostly verbal communication via the phone. No visual contact—no physical contact, so when they met on the phone their words to each other were riddled with longing and a pinch of frustration. Sometimes their daily work demands required each from time to time to encourage the other.

Roman gave soothing words of comfort and comedy when she ranted about her business. Elise peppered her language with understanding and serenity. They missed each other, they wanted each other, and they needed each other.

They were the balms for the other's soul. And as apprehensive as she should be, Elise wasn't. It had nothing to do with him being a cop. It was him—all him. Roman was one of the good guys. He was the type of man who was secure in who he was, a man who didn't have to hurt or use a woman to prove that he was Top Dog.

Elise's expression had to reveal her confusion as Roman took her gently by the arm and escorted her to the front door. "I don't know what's happened with you, Elise, but you need a slow hand, not a man who's trying to rush into you like there's not enough time to savor you, to learn you, to know you."

Elise put a few inches of space between them before she looked up at him. "How could you possibly know that about me?"

Roman focused on her well-manicured lawn for a few moments. "I'm a cop, sweetheart." He focused on her then. "I'm trained to observe, evaluate, and assess." He inched closer. "It's in the way you move sometimes—cautious, like you expect something's coming your way and you need to be prepared to run or fight."

His gaze drifted to her lips. "It's in your voice when you're not quite sure if speaking your mind is all right." Roman cupped her face in his hands. "You are beautiful, strong, and sexy—but something, some*one*, hurt you in the past to the point that you're not always sure of yourself."

He feathered his lips across hers. "I don't want to be the man who takes advantage of that. I want to be the man on the opposite end of that spectrum. The man that you'll realize is nothing like whatever or whoever hurt you."

Elise wanted to burrow into this man and nestle in his spirit. In the few months of knowing Roman, he had washed away so much turmoil in her life that Cecil had left behind.

She owed him an explanation that respected that bond he had cultivated with her. "Here's the thing, Roman—the important thing."

NALEIGHNA KAI & U. M. HIRAM

She took a long, slow breath. "I'm always cautious about who I let in my personal space—my intimate space. But somehow you slipped in under the radar without any effort. Not because you had an ulterior motive but because with you, I always feel ... all right."

She pressed her shoulder to the steel security door. "My ex-husband has a lot of money. So he felt he was ... entitled to things, entitled to treat me a certain way, entitled to take ... things I wasn't ready to give, even when I no longer lived under his roof." She let that admission hang in the air.

Roman pulled her closer and held on for several moments.

"I was tired of being afraid, tired of being used," she said softly, holding onto him. "That wall of protection has always been real for me—a survival mechanism." Elise looked up at him. "Having you with me, I *always* feel safe. A feeling I never thought I'd have again."

Roman traced a finger across her cheekbones. "I want you to always feel that way. We don't have to rush to the bedroom, we can take our time. I want to know that you're sure about this, to know that you're sure about us. I can't take the chance with my heart if you're not."

Elise locked an intense gaze on him. She fisted her tiny hands in his shirt for emphasis. "I understand where you're coming from. You can take your time if you want, but Roman ..."

His right eyebrow fanned up his forehead.

"... if you don't make love to me right now, I swear to God, I'm going to lose my freaking mind."

Roman's lips were on hers in that next instant. They were inside the door. He kicked it closed, holding her so close to him, there was no way to know where she ended and he began.

Elise had thought his previous kisses were nothing short of spectacular. But now, baby-bye. These kisses, right here, were the stuff of legend. The way he commanded her lips, her tongue, and her mouth was nothing short of earth-shattering.

"Roman," she panted.

He paused right in the middle of lowering her to the floor, and locked gazes on her.

"I don't do rug burns," she said.

Roman swept her up in his arms. "Point me in the right direction."

CHAPTER 10

Roman felt as though he was about to burst out of his skin. Good Lord, Elise not only wanted him, she ached for him as profoundly as he starved for her. Making it to the bedroom was a foggy haze. All he could focus on was her. He lowered the zipper on her form-fitting black dress and pressed a kiss to her bare shoulder. The dress hit the carpet, she turned to face him.

Elise was just sexy *all* over. She stood modeling a white lace corset with matching panties and garters anchoring black silk stockings.

"You were stunning with the dress on, but you're an absolute goddess with it off." *I'm a grown ass man, and this woman is bringing me to my knees.* "Elise?" he whispered.

"Yes?"

He was locked in a vault of awe and wonder and could not escape, and neither could his words. She smiled up at him and unbuttoned his shirt as he dropped his hands by his sides. Roman focused on his breathing as her silky hands did incredible things to the sensitive skin of his chest.

Keep it together, man. Keep it together.

A thin sheen of perspiration helped her hands travel easier across his body in more of a glide. *Hot-blooded* was the only word that came to mind.

Elise lowered her hand to the tight abs, across the flat lines of his belly, then to the buckle holding up his slacks. When the pants hit the floor, she gasped at the erection that was straining for freedom and to be into a place it had been yearning to visit ever since he had moseyed from his cruiser to her car.

Her eyes lifted to meet his and he nearly attacked.

"Happy to see me?" she teased.

"You don't know the half of it."

She slid down, taking his boxers along the way, and he stepped out of them, now completely displayed in all his golden glory.

Elise glanced up at him and the look of raw need almost killed him. For now, this was her show, her pace, her way. Roman was determined to hold firm. Then she slid slowly up his body, letting all her sweet spots, starting with her mouth, brush and graze and glide along his skin and his knees nearly buckled from just her touch.

She faced him again and crooked her finger. Roman followed like a lovesick puppy to the bed and Elise straddled him. Her thighs surrounded his hips. His hands reached out to steady her, to place her near an erection that demanded her undivided attention.

Elise snagged a condom from the nightstand, ripped it open and sheathed him.

Roman took in her beauty and wanted to see more. His hands closed around the edges of the corset and pulled it away. Her luscious heavy breasts sprang free and the need to taste was too much.

The moment his tongue flickered across those cinnamon nipples, Elise gasped. Oh, she tasted like perfection. One by one, he unlatched the hooks on the corset, then slipped off the lace panties, garters, and stockings until she was bare before him.

His hands lowered until they had a command of her buttocks, spreading her for his pleasure. He teased her pearl until she could barely catch a solid breath. He studied her reaction to everything he did. Her increasing pants encouraged him to titillate and tease.

"Roman," she gasped.

With the sound of her desperate tone, his next move was cheetah quick—flipping her so that she was under him. Elise's body arched in anticipation, demanding that he enter that sacred space.

"Elise," he said as he parted her thighs with his knee, centered himself and waited.

Her mouth sought his.

Roman let her find it and eased her ache with his tongue. When her movements increased, telling of her frustration, he lifted his head. "Are you sure," he asked trembling with his need, with hers.

"Yes," Elise cried.

Roman devoured her mouth and thrust straight to the heart of her core. She gasped and her entire body viced around every inch of him —his back, his hips, even his erection felt like her body was milking him to stay cradled within her.

He looked down at her, nervous, waiting.

"It's all right," she whispered. "It's just ... it's been a minute. That's all. I'm not fragile."

Roman slowly inched out and drove home slow and steady. He kept the pace the exact same rhythm no matter how frantically she moved beneath. Each stroke was the same measurement of completion, the same force of impact, the same intensity of sensation.

"I'm right here with you, Elise," He kept the same rhythm, never wavering. "Feel me, let it come over you," he whispered. "Let it take you. I'm right here."

Elise screamed in rapturous surrender as the floodgates to desire set her free. This was not the pulsing vibration of her climax flowing from her. No, this was the release of her pain, her fears, her past traumas. Only when those things were set free could she be truly ready for him.

He felt her damp face bury into the curve of his neck. He kept his palms splayed over her buttocks, kneading them, stroking them, bringing her to a fevered pitch.

"Roman," she panted, unable to hold on.

"That's it," he said.

"What are you doing to me, Roman?"

CHAPTER 11

"What you need me to do, baby," she heard him reply through a haze of splendor.

Elise was lost. Thrown into the eye of the storm of ecstasy. Nothing in her life had felt like this. His body was doing things to hers that she never wanted to end. When had making love ever been this earth shattering?

She clasped her hands around his face panting with aching joy. His eyes, his glorious eyes, enslaved her and then they changed to dark, sultry promises and his loving strokes change to something heady and primal and ravenous.

Elise cried out, unable to stop the storm.

"I will always give you what you need, always give you what you really want," Roman promised.

Each stroke took her to a place where all she could think about was him, having him deep within, having him touch her, having him drive her completely insane. She cried out his name, and the next series of thrusts were more demanding than the last, as if he was erasing all traces of anyone else.

Another orgasm slammed into her, and she screamed until he

NALEIGHNA KAI & U. M. HIRAM

silenced her with another kiss. Roman kept his lips on hers until nothing remained but whimpers of pleasure.

He lowered her hand to the base of his hardened member, and she gave it a gentle squeeze to keep him hard, to keep him from ending things much too soon.

"Roman?"

"We've got all night, baby. I'm going to take my time with you."

She didn't know if that was a promise or a threat. But one thing she did know, Roman Montgomery was going to make good on it either way.

* * *

SATURDAY, 8:32 a.m.

Elise lay in Roman's arms, listening to that mellow, even breathing that signaled he was taking a much-deserved rest. Between the work he did with teens who were almost destined for a life within the prison system, and taking on new cases, he always seemed to be burning the candle at both ends and striking a match to the middle.

After Cecil, and what her family had put her through, she'd thought she wouldn't allow herself to get close to anyone again. But she was more open with Roman than she had been with anyone. Truthfully, the feeling was nothing short of intoxicating.

She stroked a hand gently across his chest. He stirred and pulled her closer to him. She stopped thinking and surrendered to the comfort of being with him.

No worries. He brought peace and a sense of security to her life.

She closed her eyes, and that was her last conscious thought.

* * *

A FEW HOURS later the doorbell rang, startling her from a sound sleep.

Roman stirred, lifting up on an elbow as he looked down at her.

"I don't know who that could be," she said, answering his unspoken question.

She hurried out of bed, grabbed a robe from the closet and was down the stairs just as the bell sounded a third time.

"Just a minute," she called out.

Elise opened the door, and a pint-sized version of herself was holding a small suitcase and giving her the brightest smile. He rushed into her arms.

"Mommy! Daddy says I can come home now." Her son ducked under Elise's arms and scrambled into the living room.

"You can't come in right now," Elise said when Cecil tried to push past her any way and into her living room.

"We need to talk," he growled, obviously frustrated that she had not moved out of the way. "Donna's pregnant, and your little brat's giving her all sorts of problems."

He took off his blazer and hat and tossed them on the sofa as if he had the right to do so. "He's always demanding to see you, and—" He looked over Elise's shoulder. "Who the hell is that?"

"Mommy has a friend," her son supplied, his head tilting upward, trying to get a good look at the man making his way to the first floor landing.

Elise tracked Cecil's scan of her appearance, her disheveled hair, and her guest's sudden appearance from upstairs. His expression darkened with anger.

She could not help the smile that turned up the corners of her mouth.

That's right, I have happily moved on. Oh, and the next time we meet in court, it will be on equal footing.

"Actually," Roman announced to her son. "Mommy's friend is going to take you both out for breakfast. Would you like that, Jordan?"

"Yes, sir," her little man piped in gleefully.

Looks like Donna still hasn't learned how to cook.

Roman focused on Elise and added, "We'll have to stop by the station on the way out."

"Station?" Cecil frowned, rising from the sofa, dripping with disdain. "You're a *fireman*?"

"Police officer."

"Oooooh," Jordan cooed, tugging Roman's half-buttoned shirt. "That's what I want to be when I grow up."

"And that's a good thing," Roman said, tweaking the tip of Jordan's nose. "That means you'll always try to do what's right, especially when it comes to protecting the people you love." He said it to her son, but he locked a steely gaze on Cecil. "You know, like making sure people don't overstep their bounds or overstay their welcome."

Elise stepped over to Jordan as Roman snatched Cecil's items from the back of the suede sofa and held them out to him. "Common courtesy means calling before you show up at someone's home. The door is right behind you. Make good use of it."

Cecil glared at him for a long moment, then yanked the items from Roman's hands. He gave Elise one last, blistering look before storming from her home.

Roman watched Cecil until he reached his car and sped off. "If I've overstepped my bounds, I apologize," he said when he turned to face her. Roman crossed the distance between them and pulled her into his arms. "He needs to know that this is one place he doesn't have free rein. This place is off limits. *You* are off limits whether I'm here or not. Whether I'm … with you or …"

Elise wiggled from his embrace and looked directly into his solemn eyes. "You'll be here, Roman," she whispered, placing a hand to his cheek. "You'll be with me."

The sudden change in him floored Elise. Those simple words had brought him such relief, it was a living entity. She rose up and gave him a kiss on the cheek.

When they separated, they were blushing because it had dawned on them that they were not alone. As one, they turned to Jordan who looked at them in innocent wonder.

Roman cleared his throat. "I'll keep this little guy busy while you get dressed. Maybe I could take you and your future law officer for a quick tour of the station before breakfast." His gaze swept to the science project in Jordan's hand. "Then maybe the planetarium?"

"Yessss," Jordan crowed, pumping his fist in the air.

Elise embraced her son and looked up at Roman, mouthing the words, "Thank you."

Roman pressed a kiss to her forehead and said, "The pleasure's all mine."

SUGAR AIN'T SO SWEET

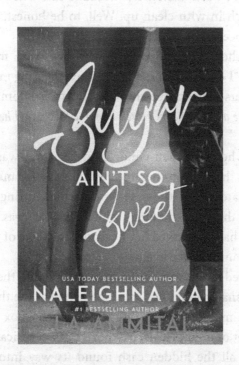

I will die if I stay here ...

Shannon's entire family sat at the dinner table enjoying a meal which took her three hours to prepare, while she mowed the jungle of their front yard, seething the entire time. She stopped to empty the bag but froze when her mother-in-law's voice carried from the open pantry window, "I had to fake a damn heart attack to make this stupid heifer get with the program."

Faked a heart attack? Wait. What?

Monique Hallerin had faked that entire one-month ordeal so Shannan would take over the daunting task of shopping, preparing, cooking, then serving Sunday dinners for fifteen people every week, only to criticize nearly everything that Shannan did. Faked it so Shannan's husband, Zach, would pick up the slack on her bills. All while her brothers-in-law and most of her children parked their lazy behinds at the dining room table every Sunday and didn't lift a finger to help. Shannan was way past tired—exhausted was a better word.

"Guests don't wash dishes," her husband said when she mentioned they could pitch in with clean up. Well, to be honest, neither did he and he hadn't been a guest since they'd said, "I do."

What she should've said on the day they were married, fifteen years ago was, "I don't," then ran past his overbearing mother and four shiftless brothers then out the church doors to freedom.

"I had to fake a damn heart attack to make this stupid heifer get with the program."

Shannan, who had seven children of her own, was now responsible for duties that her mother-in-law had done for most of her non-married life; catering to those grown ass men sitting at her dining room table at this very moment while Shannan was outside doing something she had first asked her husband, then one of them, to do.

Rage hit Shannan full force.

She staggered away from the mower, rushed into the house, ran up the stairs and snatched up her tote. She halted at the threshold of her bedroom for a moment, extracting the small shoebox in the back of the closet. A set of credit cards, passport, birth certificate, social security card, and all the hidden cash found its way into the tote. She glanced at the summer wardrobe spilling over into Zach's side and decided there wasn't anything she wanted to take. She tipped down the rear stairway into the kitchen, snatched the keys from a hook near the door to put as much distance between herself and those people as possible.

Shannan only vaguely heard the youngest of her seven children call her name. Her heart constricted as she ignored them, tears blinding her as she slid behind the wheel of an SUV that was almost a second home. Basketball. Volleyball. Football. Gymnastics. PTA. Never any breaks between or any time for her to simply breathe.

I will die if I stay here.

Those seven words came to mind, summarizing her current status. Something that first hit her when she had the argument with Zach before his family arrived ...

"No, my brothers shouldn't have to wash a dish in my house," Zachary had protested without bothering to look up from the current prosthetics project spread out over the basement. *"My mother spent a week in the hospital and she can't handle it anymore. This dinner is how we stay close. I don't see what the problem is."*

"The problem is, that it's all too much," she replied, putting aside her own work on the latest puzzle she was creating for the daily newspaper to focus more on the conversation that was long overdue. *"I'm beginning to dread Sundays. I don't have any day of rest."*

"Well, if you gave up that job you've been playing at then you wouldn't be so tired all the time," he quipped.

"I shouldn't have to give up anything," she shot back. He'd always considered the six figures she made from being a Master Cruciverbalist—crossword puzzle creator—frivolous. His career as a prosthetist brought in just under what she did. There had been a bone of contention on that score.

"Then it looks like you're going to be busy." Zachary shrugged. *"You'll be alright."*

"Wouldn't have to be so busy if you and the boys helped around here," she countered.

"My mother raised five boys on her own and never complained," he said, keeping his focus on the circuitry in his hands.

"And she was on her own because she ran your father off," she replied. *"Let's be real about that."*

Zachary's face twisted into a mask of annoyance as he glared at her. "I can't talk about this with you."

"I'm done talking. I'm tired," she snapped. "There's going to come a time when I say to hell with it."

Zach paused at the end of the wooden bench, scoffing as he asked, "And where are you going to go? Who's going to be a father to seven children?"

"They have a father," she said, and the sorrow of her reality was heavy indeed. "I need a husband."

The moment Shannan hit the expressway, she wiped her tears with the back of a trembling hand. A startling thought hit her. She could not leave her baby girl in that house.

Download it on Amazon: https://bit.ly/SugaraintsosweetU

LOVING ALL OF ME

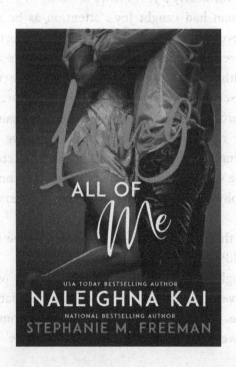

Something about him sent a delicious shiver of anticipation up Joy's spine. That shiver did a little curtsy at the base of her neck, before sliding down and sending a tingle between her thighs. Her lips parted of their own accord as if to speak, but no sound would come. The Welcome Circle, where all the rules were laid out for the total strangers embarking on an unforgettable journey, had already started.

"Rule one ... pajamas stay on the whole time," the flaxen-haired host said.

Desperate. The one word centered in Joy's mind followed by a few more. *How desperate did a woman have to be to attend an event simply to experience someone else's non-sexual touch?* She was here, wasn't she? Settled on a sofa in a room filled with people who had come for one purpose—a Cuddle Party, the new wave of safe adult interaction. Everyone played by the same set of rules. The word "no" was met with a comforting phrase, "Thank you for taking care of yourself."

Joy, a single of mother of two, had held onto the article from the *Chicago Red Eye* for nearly a year before deciding to give it a try.

The gentleman had caught Joy's attention as he swept into the room. He removed a large bottle of Southern Comfort from a brown paper bag and set it on the counter as he settled into a spot near the front door. With his back against the wall, he observed the people spread out in several open rooms. The man was stunningly handsome, with piercing brown eyes, and dark silky hair with a small shock of silver right at the widow's peak. His olive skin had been kissed by the sun, and lips that were the most delectable she'd ever laid eyes on. He wore silk, navy-blue pajamas that complimented his tall, muscular physique. She, along with several others, couldn't help but stare.

"Rule two," their host continued. "You don't have to cuddle with anyone at a cuddle party. Ever."

Oddly enough, Joy expected a place filled with outcasts, people who might have been easily overlooked on the dating scene and everywhere else. Not so. Each man was more handsome than the last. The women were either drop-dead gorgeous or girl-next-door beautiful.

The mysterious stranger remained near the door until it was his turn to share his expectations of the event. The panther-like gait commanded everyone's attention as he sauntered to the center of the living room where everyone was assembled.

"My name is Ali Khan," the smooth, baritone sound beckoned Joy from her thoughts. His voice was as sultry as his appearance, and that was saying something.

The moment his intense gaze met hers, any misgivings she'd felt about being there quickly dissipated.

"I'm here because I love the concept, and the rules. There's a freedom here that's sorely lacking in the world."

As more guests finished their introductions, Joy found that a surprising number of women shared one common thread—molestation, childhood abuse, sexual harassment. Their willingness to share something so personal gave Joy the strength she needed to let her guard down—but only a little.

She glanced at Ali again. One of the rules drifted into the forefront of her mind. *If you mean yes, say "Yes." If you mean no, say "No." If you mean "Maybe," say no. You can always change your mind later.*

Without warning, Ali turned his head and stared at Joy. They were connected across the expanse of the room for several seconds before she broke contact and lowered her eyes. Her pulse raced as if she'd run a marathon mile at top speed, and everything within Joy screamed that if asked, she'd give this man an absolute, "Hell yes."

https://bit.ly/LovingallofMeU

QUEEN OF WILMETTE

Alarms from every corner of Second Chance Safe Haven's security areas blared and echoed throughout the building. The young man with a blend of fear and confusion etched in his face yanked on the side doors of the center trying to gain access. A state-of-the-art system had been installed with three dimensional cameras with artificial intelligence scanning capabilities. As Milan and her day staff were preparing to change shifts, the teenager had rushed up to the doors, looking over his shoulders as though being chased by someone or something, tears streaming down his cheeks.

"Help me, please," he screamed. In the distance, he could see two jeeps closing in on his location. Both vehicles were each loaded with four armed occupants.

Without a second thought, Milan ran to the East door with a member of the security staff right alongside her. As if by divine intervention, she'd been able to view everything on the security cameras. Instinctively, cries for help were on her radar and tugged at her heart strings. The center was built on the foundation of making a difference in the life of the country's disadvantaged and underprivileged youth, both young women and men.

"What's your name?" she asked in what she hoped was a soothing voice as soon as they pulled him safely inside the building.

Out of breath and perspiring so hard his drenched shirt was plastered against his pale skin, "Jonathan Reinhart."

Milan peered at him. "Jonathan, why are you in such a panic?"

Wiping his eyes with the back of a trembling right hand, he looked up at her, "They want me to fight to overthrow our government, I can't do that. I don't believe in their cause. So, I ran, my mother said I would be safe here."

Pausing, then taking a deep calming breath, Milan processed his words. "Who wants you to fight and for what cause?"

He tensed up and grew eerily quiet, self-preservation mode. She would have to take a different approach to get him to open up. Tonight, she'd make sure he was provided shelter. Tomorrow they'd find out more about this young man.

Once Milan made sure he was settled in a room and ate a meal of flatbread and minced lamb meat, she left him in the capable hands of her evening staff. At least two male employees were always on each shift to ensure safety and provide that extra layer of internal security.

Because of the work they did, neighboring countries sought to close down the center. Thankfully, they were under the protection of the Durabian government and Kings of the Castle. She'd be back the following day and put her social work training into play to start building trust with their unexpected new resident.

Thirty minutes later, Milan grabbed a bottled water from the second shelf of her fridge. After taking some time to breathe, she slid into a shower to release some of the tension that built up throughout the day. Briefly, she thought about the young man who had seemingly fought his way to get to the center for protection. At least that was his claim. Tonight, he would be safe until they could verify his story.

Standing on the master bedroom balcony, Milan looked out at the beautiful Durabian skyline from the second level of her home. The six bedroom, seven bath mini mansion was located in a gated community that housed a number of their Castle family members. Peacefulness surrounded her as she closed her eyes and breathed in the fresh, crisp air.

Her thoughts shifted to the decisions she was forced to make concerning Second Chance Safe Haven. The launch and operations of the center were her baby. Its ultimate goal was to provide services such as educational training and a shelter to the individuals who were housed inside the facility. They were on the borders near Nadaum and the United Arab Emirates, in a span of six months their clientele had grown beyond anything originally planned.

With all of the unrest happening in neighboring countries, there'd been an influx of teens looking for a secure place. Milan's mission was to help as many of them as possible. Her own personal experience fueled this passion because she knew all too well the feeling of abandonment. Her mind flashed back to the day that her mother kicked her out of the house.

"Better get you one of them dope boys, worry about schooling later," Pearline said.

Shaking in anger with balled up fists, Milan shot back. "Wasn't daddy one of those dope boys? When does he get out of prison? What's him being in prison done for you?"

Pearline's anger got the best of her, and she was standing inches away from her youngest daughter. "Are you sassing me?"

"Just stating facts. Grandma said the minute a woman puts her faith solely in a man to take care of her is when she gives up every ounce of her power."

"Well, Wonder Woman, lasso your little brown ass upstairs and pack your shit. How's that for power?"

Even though her aunt tried to step in and stop what was happening, Milan went upstairs to grab her belongings. The last words that she spoke before walking out of the door and never looking back were, "One day, Mama, you're going to need me."

Ironically, her siblings were having babies, failing in school, or participating in some form of illegal activities. Her mother didn't achieve her personal dreams and placed the blame on having children. Most of her anger was aimed directly at her youngest daughter who never landed in any type of trouble. Inhaling and then exhaling a deep breath, Milan let all those troubling memories escape her mind, at least momentarily.

Refocusing her energy on the current issues in Durabia, she put her gaze on the table occupied by her laptop, notepad, binder, and calculator. Working through the phases she'd implement along with costs for the additions to the center were a top priority. More rooms and valued added services for the teens, totally in compliance with Durabian customs, as well as increased staffing.

Once again, she took in the peaceful horizon, envisioning the changes and upgrades that would be implemented but her mind strayed to the political tight rope she walked as well. One of the advantages working in her favor is that the center was self-funded. They didn't need to depend on governmental financial support to operate, even though there were strict guidelines to follow. She was an American, connected to Durabian royalty through Vikkas, her high school sweetheart. Although the facility was kept under the radar, for obvious reasons, word seemed to be getting around about its existence. That could bring danger to their doorstep. And it came in a form that they weren't prepared to handle.

KING OF DURABIA

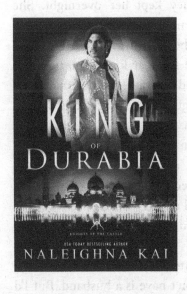

"You risked your life for my grandson," Sheikh Aayan said, his voice echoing through the ornate throne room. "Ask for anything and I will see what can be done."

Ellena scanned the expectant faces of the throngs of people who had gathered for this unexpected audience with the ruler of Durabia. Most of their tunics and dishdashas differed from her casual attire of a simple white blouse and black slacks. "Thank you, but that isn't necessary. I did what anyone would do."

"Evidently, not everyone," he said, and his angry glare focused on the bodyguard, caregivers, and everyone who had stood by when Javed, the little royal, had swept past Ellena and landed on the moving conveyor belt.

All of them had frozen in place the moment Javed brushed against the rubber bounding strip and was sucked into the void. The video of

Ellena dropping her tote bag, diving in after him, and cradling him in her arms as they were both tossed through the maze of steel and vinyl, all while being battered by suitcases and duffel bags alike, went viral.

Ellena had closed her eyes, bracing under each blow. Javed's laughter was a stark contrast to her pain. The cameras caught everything, including the tail end of the journey when Ellena tumbled out of the final drop onto another belt and finally into the metal cart that would carry the luggage onto the plane. Security finally found their legs and scrambled to make it to Ellena and the little boy before they sustained further injuries. Well, before she did. Her fleshy body was all the protection that Javed needed.

Javed Khan, a great grandson of the Royal Family, was completely unharmed. Ellena, on the day of arrival for a class reunion vacation, had to be rushed to the hospital. They kept her overnight. She sustained a few cuts and bruises that matched the dent in her ego when the entire world saw her tossed head over ass multiple times. And when the adrenaline wore off and the fear kicked in, the little royal refused to let her go. He even had to travel in the emergency transport with her because none of the guards or caregivers managed to force him to release his hold on Ellena.

Now she stood in a palace situated in the heart of a metropolis in the Middle East with a décor that was unrivaled by anything she'd ever seen. Gold—everything was layered with it—the walls, doors, accented by purples and reds that added a sultry warmth to all of the opulence of the furniture, paintings, and draperies covering massive windows.

"Well, to be honest, I haven't wanted much," she said with a nervous laugh. "And the only thing I don't have is a husband. But I'd love to have a place here in Durabia, where I can come and go as I please. If that is at all possible."

"Done," the Sheikh said, beckoning to the man who had visited the hospital twice to see about her condition. "Kamran, come."

"Wait. What?" She laughed and rested a hand on her ample bosom. "An apartment, really?"

"Your new husband," he answered with a grand gesture that would have made Vanna White proud. "This is my oldest son."

The man was drop-dead gorgeous. Olive complexion, dark hair, goatee neatly trimmed to perfection, and piercing brown eyes that missed nothing. He was more suited to a fashion runway than a palace. Truthfully, she wasn't sure if it was the tunics, neat beards, head coverings or what. Durabia seemed to have no shortage of handsome men. But the Sheikh's son was a masterpiece, exuding the kind of confidence that came with a man who was certain of his place in the world. His gaze swept across her face with a complexion slightly darker than his olive tone, then quickly covered the distance over her curves, then his lips lifted in a warm, appreciative smile that practically lit up his dark brown eyes and sent heat straight to places that had been dormant since the Queen of Sheba caused King Solomon to lose his entire mind.

Ellena shook her head, clearing her mind of all manner of wickedness that came after that wonderful assessment. "I think you misunderstood. I was joking about the husband part. The apartment, time share or whatever you call them here, that's all I really want."

"You will have both," the Sheikh commanded with a nod of finality no one would dare to question. "A husband and a place here. My son needs a wife and you mentioned you do not have a husband. Problem solved."

"But doesn't he have to give you heirs or something?" She instinctively brought her hands near her belly. "My eggs are old enough to be married and have children of their own by now."

First, a roar of laughter went up from him. A few moments later, it was mirrored by everyone standing around her. Yes, that line was funny, but the one thing she understood was the unfairness of the situation. At least for Kamran. And that was no laughing matter.

The Sheikh waved away that thought. "That will not be a concern. He is unable to give you or any woman children. And a woman of African descent will never sit on the Durabian throne. We are safe on that score."

A shadow of sadness flickered in Kamran's eyes and his skin

flushed a shade darker. Ellena tried to read a deeper meaning into his father's words. She still came up with *unfair*. "So, you just throw him to a random woman because he can't give you an heir? He is *still* a man. He *still* has value," she insisted. "A brain, intelligence, and a purpose." She inhaled, trying to tamp down on her anger. "The apartment is fine, Sheikh. Thank you, but I will not be foisted on a man who has no say in the matter. That's downright cruel."

A gasp came from the core of people around them before silence descended in the room. Even Kamran flinched.

The Sheikh's face darkened with anger as he slowly came to his feet. "Are you refusing—"

"Give me nine days—"

All eyes focused on the handsome man, who left his father's side and moseyed toward her like some type of Arabian cowboy. All swagger, no gun necessary.

"Give me nine days," he repeated and moved across the expensive Persian carpet until he stood in front of her, towering over her near six-foot height by three inches of his own. "Nine days for me to show you Durabia, to answer any questions you may have. To let you explore the place, the people, the culture. Then you decide."

Ellena found it hard to catch her breath. The man was so virile she felt warm all the way to her follicles. "Nine days? I have to go home. I have a job back there. I used all of my vacation and two of my sick days for this trip."

"Your job?" he asked, frowning as though he couldn't fathom what the word meant.

"Yes. A job. Nine to five. Benefits. All of that. You know, what regular folks do to keep an address."

Kamran remained silent for a few moments as he peered at her. "How much do they pay you?"

She winced, then flickered a gaze to his right and felt the intensity of everyone's attention. "It doesn't matter."

"How much?" He beckoned for her to come nearer. "Whisper it to me."

Ellena hesitated a moment, then complied, moving so close she inhaled the intoxicating scent of sandalwood. She managed to whisper an answer, then inched back to put a little distance between them.

"For the rest of your life?" he asked, his tone and wide eyes reflecting the incredulity registered in his facial expression.

"Until I'm sixty-seven and retire," she replied, daunted by his tone. "But there's also health benefits and other factors that I can't put a number on."

Kamran blinked as though doing a set of mental calculations and coming up with what probably amounted to simple interest on his bank account. "Give me the particulars and I will wire the money into your account."

She parted her lips to protest but he held up a hand. "Saying yes to taking me as your husband is still your choice. With this, I am simply ensuring your peace of mind. And as a gift for your kindness, your selflessness in saving a child who was a stranger to you."

Ellena let out a long, slow breath, because staying here permanently, marrying him, would be a lost cause. She loved her job as a personal assistant at Vantage Point. Alejandro Reyes, a "Fixer" of everything from political and corporate espionage, to terrorist attacks, was the absolute best person to work for. And she loved the predictability of her life. Traveling overseas was the most adventurous event in her life. Still, curiosity won out over common sense and she said, "All right. Thank you."

"Now we go about the business of getting to know one another," he said, smiling as though her consent brought him much pleasure. Evidently, he wanted this to happen and the intensity of his gaze bore into her soul. "So that you can make an informed decision, yes?"

She glanced over his shoulder, taking in some of the envious looks a few of the women tried to hide. "Why are you doing this?" she asked him. "Why are you allowing them to serve you up to some foreign woman as if you do not have value?"

"Because I recognize this is God's will," he answered. "And who am I to leave a precious gift unwrapped?"

Her eyebrows drew in, as she tried to decipher the hidden

meaning behind his words. The man had a peaceful, confident air but also a playful vibe about him.

"Yes, that was a double entendre." His smile widened and she could swear the heavens opened up and smiled with him.

Good Lord, I'm in trouble.

Download it on Amazon: https://bit.ly/KingofDurabia1

LOVING ME FOR ME

"With all of those degrees," Devesh Maharaj countered. "I'm sure you're very much aware of the numbers. Black women outnumber Black men nearly three to one. More if you count the ones who are not available to them—married, in jail, gay, or those who don't want to commit to marriage."

The audience clapped, the more enthusiastic applause coming from Black women.

"They'll go to their graves while waiting for the Black man who God's supposed to mysteriously recycle so she can have her turn," Devesh said. "He took two fish and five loaves of bread, and it became enough to feed a multitude. But I never heard of Him using His power of multiplication to create extra brothers when there are already so many other desirable seeds. Those seeds on the ground might at least bloom into a relationship that is more than a placeholder until a good Black man mysteriously comes along. And it might be the best thing that's ever happened for both of them."

This time the audience whooped, hollered, and laughed and Sharon placed an encouraging hand on his shoulder. Sheryl nodded and had an ear-splitting smile.

Shawn's face darkened with anger. "So now you speak for Black women?"

"I don't have to speak for Black women because I only have to focus on one woman." He took a sip from the coffee mug and returned it on the coaster. "A woman I love, a woman whose spirit I'm not going to crush just to satisfy my ego. You have a wife—she's your business. I have my wife—she's my business. I'm not all up in your finances. I'm not all up in your bedroom." From the corner of his eye, Devesh saw Sheryl and Sara nodding and putting the evil eye on Shawn. "Your ego took pleasure in hurting Reign. I take pleasure in helping my woman to heal."

"My woman?" Shawn examined Reign before looking back to Devesh. "Sounds like some cave man white boy mess."

"Number one, I'm not White, I'm East Indian. And my second point is too many men have used the word wife in a way that implies property. Saying my woman is primal, instinctual." Devesh's smile disappeared as his eyes narrowed to slits when they focused on Shawn. "It means I will nail someone's balls to the wall if they come at her the wrong way."

"Are you threatening me? On live television?" Shawn said, shoulders stiffening.

"Not threatening anyone. I'm going to need you to keep my woman's name out of your mouth." Devesh leaned in, causing Shawn to slide back. "See, you're not upset about the most important part of the equation. You're upset about the money. If I wasn't rolling in it right now, you wouldn't blink about who I chose as my mate." Devesh wagged a finger in Shawn's direction. "So my brother, you're going to have to stay mad—I mean the next seventy years worth of mad, because I'm going to be loving my woman until there's no more love to be had."

PERSISTENCE

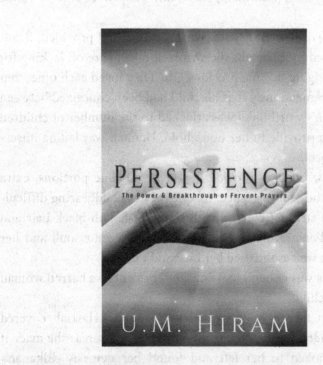

One man, two wives.

Children laughed and played outside under the clear, sunny skies of Ephraim; a small town located thirteen miles northeast of the capital city of Jerusalem. Hillsides served as a backdrop for their mischief. Adolescent young men were playing tag, throwing rocks, and wrestling one another. Their liveliness filled the atmosphere, while the young ladies sat nearby admiring their own simple, beautiful attire and watching the action.

Enjoyable and sometimes nerve-wracking sounds traveled throughout the courtyard. They served as constant reminders that one woman was able to provide her husband heirs, while the other was not. A daunting, heart wrenching experience. Elkanah, Hannah, and Peninnah shared a life, but they were not parallel. The scale was visibly unbalanced. A continual reminder of a seemingly unanswered prayer.

How could anyone coexist in this space?

Resentment, disappointment, strife, and envy were sure to reside —and they did.

Hannah's desires went beyond what her husband provided. Beautiful and favored by Elkanah, she was well taken care of, lacking for nothing. Yet longing for one precious gift. They loved each other, but it pained her tremendously that no child had been conceived between them. A woman's worthiness was attached to the number of children she was able to provide to her household. Hannah was failing miserably in that aspect.

Despite this, Elkanah showed her favor. Double portions, extra affection, and the utmost respect in spite of her childbearing difficulties. She was a striking woman with shoulder-length black hair and flawless skin. Penetrating brown eyes bore into your soul, and her figure fueled as well as satisfied her husband's desire.

None of this was enough to bring contentment to a barren woman yearning for a child.

Deciding to take a walk around the grounds, Hannah covered herself and headed towards the front entrance. As soon as she made it outside, she looked to her left and found her nemesis—Elkanah's second wife Peninnah—sitting there. It seemed today the entire household wanted to get out and enjoy the beautiful weather. Before she could turn in the other direction, Peninnah stood and walked boldly in her direction.

Bracing herself for the unwelcome interaction, Hannah silently took a deep breath. She wasn't scared of this woman by any means. She merely desired to be left alone and not antagonized. Silently praying, she refused to allow this woman's festered unhappiness to upend her peacefulness. Determined to keep a neutral posture, Hannah stood strong and didn't flinch when her space was invaded by the unwanted presence.

"Where are you heading? Are you finally leaving us?" Peninnah demanded. Her posture was adversarial, her tone full of malice. Every time she opened her mouth, the surrounding air became stagnant. No greeting, just straight to an episode of bullying. Happiness seemed to evade this woman.

"And why would I be leaving my home?" Hannah replied calmly.

"Your home?" she spat. "I think the presence of me and my children are the only things making this place a home for Elkanah."

"Considering I was here and settled before you arrived, this is and always will be my dwelling place."

Peninnah rolled her eyes, saying "You're childless and taking up space. While you may do your best to keep Elkanah satisfied in other ways, there's one main area you're lacking in. So again, why are you here?"

The second wife often ridiculed Hannah, belittling and antagonizing her at every given opportunity. She was a constant thorn in Hannah's side. Feeling superior to Hannah, Peninnah felt it was her right to be an oppressor. Her jealousy was swift and deadly, like a speeding freight train.

Why?

It was obvious she felt she'd proven her worth as a woman. After all, she was the one who'd given their husband ten sons and two daughters. She alone was ensuring that Elkanah's bloodline continued on strong. On the flip side of that, Peninnah did feel envious that kindness and unconditional love was shown to someone she felt wasn't worthy of those honors. Wrath and animosity saturated the heart of Hannah's adversary.

The woman's voice was annoying. She was a nuisance who sucked up the air in her occupied space. Continuous hatred seeped from her pores. Peninnah was a beautiful landscape on the outside. Darkness and strife claimed residence internally.

Hannah was aware of her own beauty, but never flaunted it. She was modest in nature and kind to everyone. It appeared her warmth didn't do much to foster a peaceful existence with Peninnah. The woman was ruthless and unsympathetic to Hannah's plight.

"Did you not hear me?" Peninnah spewed venomously. "I asked you a question."

Looking at the woman as if she'd lost all her marbles, Hannah didn't respond, knowing this was the onset of a browbeating session. This woman pushed all of her buttons. But never wanting to carry hatred in her heart, Hannah wouldn't lash back; she'd just turn her feelings inward.

"I know you understand me. What's the matter? Are you going to cry again?" Peninnah snickered.

Taking a deep breath, Hannah replied smoothly, "I belong here as much as you do. Let me remind you again, I was here first and will remain for a very long time. So, you can think on that and continue to be your wonderful, hate-filled self."

She did her best to stay positive. Her faith was unbreakable, her prayers precise. Trusting God to change the current circumstances is what she kept holding on to. However, dire sadness and disappointment would appear when Hannah was painfully reminded of her infertility.

An arched eyebrow and wicked grin preceded the poison escaping her foe's lips. "Really? Well now. Remember this: you haven't even produced one heir for our husband," Peninnah laughed. "It's taken a second wife to accomplish what you should have by now. So, you think about that."

Verbal punches flowed from her mouth like the steady flow of a river. This woman knew no boundaries, except as it pertained to the right time to strike. Always when their mate was not around, and Hannah's vulnerability was obvious.

"Elkanah loves me," Hannah spoke in a whispered tone. Though a strong, painful indicator of her angst threatened to fill her eyes, she did her best to keep up a brave face. "Is that what pains you and the reason you're so nasty towards me?"

"You are here on borrowed time. Our husband needs children, and that's the one thing you aren't able to give him," she said, placing a hand over her stomach. "My womb has been blessed. Why has the God you pray to so often punished you?"

In that moment, Hannah's spirit took a huge blow. As much as she tried to let harsh words roll off her shoulders, it was a tough thing to do. The hurt and shameful feelings surfaced quickly. Her emotions took hold.

The evil comments always caused her grief. Suffocating, self-inflicted thoughts of feeling inadequate as a woman and wife pushed her into a depressive state. Her peace was disrupted by the hostility shown courtesy of the other woman sharing her living accommodations. Though at times it was unbearable, Hannah's faith was shaken but never wavered.

Despair filled her heart. Elkanah never made her feel less than a woman. However, Peninnah was a visual reminder of what was missing in her life. Regardless of the unpleasant words spilling from this woman's mouth, Hannah stood firm in her belief that she would be blessed with a child. Hannah felt deep down the God she served was powerful and would prove that by performing a miracle in her life.

"He isn't punishing me. It has not been my time, but that day is coming. Elkanah and I will have a child," she replied adamantly.

Peninnah laughed hysterically. "Yeah, right. I think when you're old and shriveled up, you'll still be talking about the same blessings that'll never come. Face it, you are not worthy. The sooner you embrace that fact, the sooner you can move on and out."

"Your evil words will come back to haunt you. My blessings will come, and you'll be a witness despite what you're spewing."

Another round of wicked words sent Hannah into a tailspin. She turned and hurried hastily to her chambers, not allowing tears to escape her eyes.

As much anger as she felt about the wicked things Peninnah said to her, Hannah knew that praying would keep her from laying hands on that woman. Although her humbleness was seen as weakness, a fire burned inside. If unleashed, some external damage control would be needed. Her goal was to be the bigger person, not to react to negativity.

Entering her chambers, Hannah allowed herself to release the exasperation she'd been feeling. Salty tears flowed and the weight of sadness released from her soul. The human side of her battled with giving in to the anger and doubt, while the Spirit encouraged her to stand strong and keep the faith.

Food was brought to her during this time of solitude. Hours later, the sliced lamb, mixed vegetables, and baked bread were cold and untouched. The chambermaids came to take the food away, but left empty-handed, looking deeply concerned about her well-being. Few words were spoken, which was unlike their normal interactions. Hannah knew they would relay this to Elkanah, and it would only be a matter of time before he showed up to her chambers.

ABOUT NALEIGHNA KAI

Naleighna Kai is the *USA TODAY, Essence®*, and national bestselling and award-winning author of several controversial women's fiction, contemporary fiction, Christian fiction, Romance, Suspense, and Science Fiction novels that plumb the depth of unique love triangles and women's issues. She is also a contributor to a New York Times bestseller, one of AALBC's 100 Top Authors, a member of the Chicago Vocational School Hall of Fame (CVS), Mercedes Benz Mentor Award Nominee, and the E. Lynn Harris Author of Distinction.

In addition to successfully cracking the code of landing a deal for herself and others with a major publishing house, she continues to "pay it forward" with the experience of NK Tribe Called Success, the Kings of the Castle Series, the Knights of the Castle Series, and by organizing the annual Cavalcade of Authors which gives readers intimate access to the most accomplished writing talent today. She resides in Chicago where she is working on her next two books.

ABOUT U. M. HIRAM

U.M. Hiram is a #1 Bestselling Author, Book Coach, and Interior Book Designer who currently resides in Kansas. She is also a human resource professional and 21-year retired Navy veteran writing in multi-genres that include Christian Fiction/Inspirational, Memoir, and Romance.

Her two latest releases are #1 Amazon Bestselling Persistence: The Power & Breakthrough of Fervent Prayer, Book #8 in the Merry Hearts Inspirational Book Series and Queen of Wilmette, Book #7 in the Queens of the Castle Series.

Reading, traveling, watching sports, and spending time with her family is what she enjoys doing the most when not putting pen to paper.

Website: https://authorumhiram.com/

Printed in the USA
CPSIA information can be obtained
at www.ICGtesting.com
LVHW031917110823
754841LV00010B/1102